I LOVE MY MOMMY BECAUSE...

Laurel Porter-Gaylord

pictures by
Ashley Wolff

DUTTON CHILDREN'S BOOKS   NEW YORK

In loving memory of Ruth Irene Porter
and Barbara Whitney Gaylord

L. P. G.

For Granny Deane

A. W.

Library of Congress Cataloging-in-Publication Data
Porter-Gaylord, Laurel.
   I love my mommy because—/by Laurel Porter-Gaylord; illustrated
by Ashley Wolff.—1st ed.
      p.   cm.
   Summary: Familiar phrases from a preschooler's world give
a child's-eye view of being an animal baby. Many different
animal mothers are shown caring for their young.
   ISBN 0-525-44625-7
   [1. Mother and child—Fiction.]   I. Wolff, Ashley, ill.
II. Title.
PZ7.P836.Iaab   1991
[E]—dc20   90-2792   CIP   AC

Published in the United States by
Dutton Children's Books,
a division of Penguin Books USA Inc.

Designer: Barbara Powderly
Printed in Hong Kong
First Edition   10 9 8 7 6 5 4 3 2 1

The animal behavior pictured in this book
has been verified by wildlife biologists.

I love my mommy because
she reads me stories.

Cat and kitten

She listens when I talk.

She feeds me when I'm hungry.

She keeps me nice and clean.

Koala bear and joey

She takes me for a ride.

Sea lion and pup   Bottlenose dolphin and calf

I love my mommy because

Gray whale and calf

she swims with me.

Panda and cub

She gives me great big hugs.

She keeps me safe and warm.

Hen and chicks

She takes me for a walk.

She lets me play in the mud.

Elephant and calf

She is big and strong.

She comes when I call.

Raccoon and young   Skunk and young   Deer and fawn

I love my mommy because

Great horned owl and chicks

she is not afraid of the dark.

She tucks me in.

She rocks me to sleep.

I love my mommy
and my mommy loves me.